KIDS CAN'T STOP READING THE CHOOSE YOUR OWN ADVENTURE® STORIES!

'It's exciting choosing your own adventure and being the star of the story. It makes you think instead of just reading it and forgetting it'
Charlotte Walton, age 13

'Though I don't like reading much, I loved this'
Robert Gladman, age 10

'I was suffocated twice, buried alive and had a spell put on me – all in one night!'
Karen Hay, age 10

And teachers like this series, too:

'They are very popular and assist in motivating children. Pupils find them absorbing and exciting'
Mr Keith Hurst, Head of English, Frogmore School, Hampshire

CHOOSE YOUR OWN ADVENTURE® AND MAKE READING MORE FUN!

CHOOSE YOUR OWN ADVENTURE®— AND MAKE READING MORE FUN!

Bantam Books in the Choose Your Own Adventure® Series
Ask your bookseller for the books you have missed

1 THE CAVE OF TIME
2 JOURNEY UNDER THE SEA
3 BY BALLOON TO THE SAHARA
4 SPACE AND BEYOND
5 THE MYSTERY OF CHIMNEY ROCK
6 YOUR CODE NAME IS JONAH
7 THE THIRD PLANET FROM ALTAIR
8 DEADWOOD CITY
9 WHO KILLED HARLOWE THROMBEY?
10 THE LOST JEWELS OF NABOOTI
11 MYSTERY OF THE MAYA
12 INSIDE UFO 54-40
13 THE ABOMINABLE SNOWMAN
14 THE FORBIDDEN CASTLE
15 HOUSE OF DANGER
16 SURVIVAL AT SEA
17 THE RACE FOREVER
18 UNDERGROUND KINGDOM
19 SECRET OF THE PYRAMIDS
20 ESCAPE
21 HYPERSPACE
22 SPACE PATROL
23 THE LOST TRIBE
24 LOST ON THE AMAZON
25 PRISONER OF THE ANT PEOPLE
26 THE PHANTOM SUBMARINE
27 THE HORROR OF HIGH RIDGE
28 MOUNTAIN SURVIVAL
29 TROUBLE ON PLANET EARTH
30 THE CURSE OF BATTERSLEA HALL
31 VAMPIRE EXPRESS
32 TREASURE DIVER
33 THE DRAGONS' DEN
34 THE MYSTERY OF THE HIGHLAND CREST
35 JOURNEY TO STONEHENGE
36 THE SECRET TREASURE OF TIBET
37 WAR WITH THE EVIL POWER MASTER
38 SABOTAGE
39 SUPERCOMPUTER
40 THE THRONE OF ZEUS
41 SEARCH FOR THE MOUNTAIN GORILLAS

Choose Your Own Adventure Books for younger readers

1 THE CIRCUS
2 THE HAUNTED HOUSE
3 SUNKEN TREASURE
4 YOUR VERY OWN ROBOT
5 GORGA, THE SPACE MONSTER
6 THE GREEN SLIME
7 HELP! YOU'RE SHRINKING
8 INDIAN TRAIL
9 DREAM TRIPS
10 THE GENIE IN THE BOTTLE
11 THE BIGFOOT MYSTERY
12 THE CREATURE FROM MILLER'S POND
13 JUNGLE SAFARI
14 THE SEARCH FOR CHAMP
15 THE THREE WISHES
16 DRAGONS!
17 WILD HORSE COUNTRY
18 SUMMER CAMP
19 THE TOWER OF LONDON
20 TROUBLE IN SPACE
21 MONA IS MISSING
22 THE EVIL WIZARD
23 THE POLAR BEAR EXPRESS
24 THE MUMMY'S TOMB

CHOOSE YOUR OWN ADVENTURE® • 41

SEARCH FOR THE MOUNTAIN GORILLAS

BY JIM WALLACE

ILLUSTRATED BY RON WING

An R. A. Montgomery Book

BANTAM BOOKS
TORONTO • NEW YORK • LONDON • SYDNEY • AUCKLAND

RL 6, IL age 10 and up

SEARCH FOR THE MOUNTAIN GORILLAS
A Bantam Book / August 1985

Original conception by Edward Packard.

ISBN 0-553-24745-X

Published simultaneously in the United States and Canada

Bantam Books are published by Bantam Books, Inc. Its trademark, consisting of the words "Bantam Books" and the portrayal of a rooster, is registered in U.S. Patent and Trademark Office and in other countries. Marca Registrada. Bantam Books, Inc., 666 Fifth Avenue, New York, New York 10103.

Printed and bound in Great Britain by Hunt Barnard Printing Ltd.

O 0 9 8 7 6 5 4 3 2 1

For Tali, Anne,
and George Saxton

WARNING!!!

Do not read this book straight through from beginning to end! It contains many different adventures you may have as you enter a remote African wildlife preserve in search of mountain gorillas. From time to time as you read along, you will be asked to make decisions and choices. You choice may lead to success or disaster!

Only you are responsible for your fate because only you can make these decisions. After you make each choice, follow the instructions to see what happens to you next.

Think carefully before you act. Your adventures may lead to a fabulous article for your nature magazine—or to the dangers that lie hidden in the wilderness.

Good luck!

Wham! Your Land Rover slams through another gaping hole in the red dirt road. Clouds of dust swirl around you.

You are a photographer and writer for the nature magazine *African Naturalist*. You've done some excellent work on the mountain gorilla, a species that is almost extinct. Now your magazine has sent you on an expedition to a remote wildlife preserve in Uganda. You will be searching for the mountain gorillas that have been sighted there. This is the first time they've been seen in this area of Central Africa, and the reports are sketchy.

You've asked Edward Kiwanuka, a zoologist at the University of East Africa and a specialist in mountain gorillas, to join you. The preserve you're heading for is called the Impenetrable Forest. It's a few miles north of Kigezi Gorilla Sanctuary Park. Both places are on the border of the country Zaire and are on the slopes of extinct volcanoes.

You're driving. You turn to Ed. "Where do you think those gorillas in the Impenetrable Forest come from, Ed? Everyone says the few left live only in the Gorilla Sanctuary Park."

"My guess is they're fleeing the park. The park rangers haven't been able to keep herdsmen and their cattle out of the park. Uganda is a growing country, you know. The sad thing is, once the lower mountain slopes are farmed or made into pastures for cattle, the gorillas lose that precious little bit of territory. After a while they'll vanish."

Turn to page 2.

It's late afternoon. You gun the Land Rover around a hairpin turn. Roadblock! A jumble of freshly cut trees lies across the road.

Ed frowns. "Poachers probably made this mess. For years they've been coming aross the border from Zaire to hunt deer illegally in the Gorilla Sanctuary Park. Park officials have started cracking down on them. This roadblock may be their way of getting back!"

With your trail machetes, you and Ed take an

hour to hack away enough of the trees to smash the Land Rover through the roadblock. But now the sun has set. In a few minutes it'll be pitch black! There's no twilight in the tropics. You have to decide what to do.

You could camp nearby for the night. Or you could go ahead up the dark mountain road into the Impenetrable Forest and try to find the forestry outpost where Mweri, your gorilla tracker, waits. You told him you'd meet him on this day. You can't be sure he'll wait until the next.

If you decide to set up camp, turn to page 6.

If you decide to drive into the Impenetrable Forest, turn to page 12.

"We'll look for gorillas without Mweri," you tell Ed. "We can use this outpost for our base camp. If he does show up, he'll see the Land Rover and know we're here."

The trail goes up a ridge toward a towering cone-shaped volcanic peak. By instinct you cut off to the right toward a saddle-shaped area you glimpse between peaks. The leafy undergrowth is thick with wild celery—a favorite gorilla food. If gorillas have moved to the Impenetrable Forest, maybe they'll be here!

"Look, Ed!" you whisper. "Chewed celery stalks! And look here, gorillas have just passed through! All the plants are bent over, pointing in the direction they went."

Nettles sting your face, but you don't care. You creep on all fours following the traces.

Ed veers off to the left. "I'll go up into this bamboo grove. A couple of tracks go this way. Let's each whistle if we spot any gorillas," he whispers behind you.

Turn to page 8.

You and Ed put out the fire, stow the gear, and climb into your Land Rover to start for park headquarters. The taillights of Halvorsen's truck guide you through the thick darkness. No village lights shine up at you, and no roadside lights outline the steep, winding track.

He turns onto a narrower trail. You follow. This road is even more treacherous, and you concentrate on making the hairpin turns.

Finally your headlights sweep past the park gates, and Halvorsen stops by a large house situated under some flowering trees.

Turn to page 10.

You decide to set up camp for the night. About half a mile along the dark road, your headlights shine on a large rock.

"Let's pitch our tent here, behind that rock. We can have a small cooking fire, too," you say.

"Right," says Ed. "It's a good spot. No one coming along the road could see us." You hide the Land Rover and start setting up camp.

As Ed is passing you a bowl of the stew he's cooked over the wood fire, a deep screaming cuts through the night insect noises.

"*Wraaaah! Mmreee!*" It echoes and rises and falls in a distinct rhythm. You and Ed stare into the dark. Then you realize what the sound is.

"Oh, a chain saw!" You laugh in relief. "It's back at the roadblock. I'm going there, Ed. Give me twenty minutes, and if I'm not back, come for me."

After walking half a mile, you come upon a truck parked in the road. The roadblock has been cleared away. In the lights of the truck, you see two men stowing a chain saw.

"Well, Jonathan," says one of the men to the other, "we'll have to use that old abandoned mine road to the park if those fool poachers keep messing this one up! Let's go."

On impulse you walk into the light.

Turn to page 115.

You decide to wait for the rain to pass. It finally tapers off into mist, but drops of water continue to fall from the drapes of moss that hang from the tree branches. It's cold!

Two gorillas leave their tree trunk shelter and begin to strip *Galium* leaves from their vines and eat them. As they move slowly toward you, you recognize them. They are the baby who's always causing mischief with the adults and its mother.

You snap several pictures of the mother. She wads the *Galium* leaves into a ball before she pops them into her mouth. The youngster tries to copy the procedure, but its ball unwinds before it gets it to its mouth. In frustration the baby jumps up and down in a little dance and pokes its mother.

Crash! From far off come the sounds of voices and people thrashing around in the undergrowth. The group's silverback leader roars a warning to his family and stares in the direction of the disturbance.

Turn to page 55.

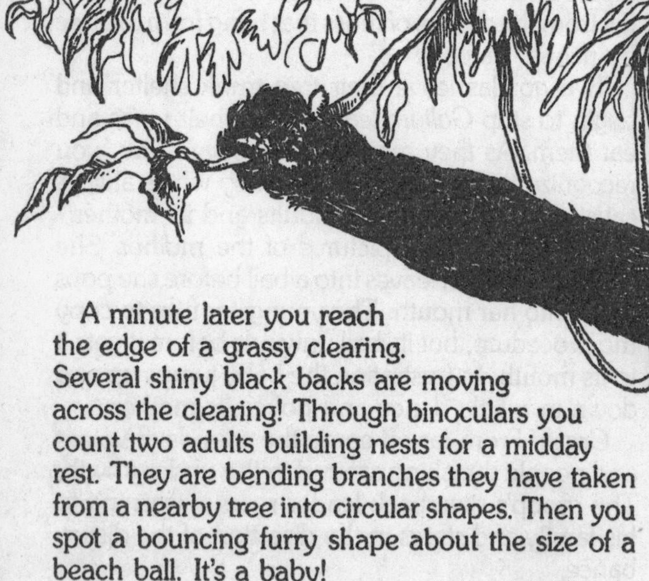

A minute later you reach the edge of a grassy clearing. Several shiny black backs are moving across the clearing! Through binoculars you count two adults building nests for a midday rest. They are bending branches they have taken from a nearby tree into circular shapes. Then you spot a bouncing furry shape about the size of a beach ball. It's a baby!

The baby is climbing all over the back of the largest gorilla you've ever seen. His back is distinctly silver colored. Only mature males are this color; he's probably the leader of this family group. He rolls over onto his back, lounging in his resting nest. He makes a good-natured rumbling sound at the baby as it jumps all over his stomach and chest.

Before you can whistle to Ed, you hear a scream. "Help! Help! Quick!"

Turn to page 102.

9

Early the next morning you and Ed have breakfast on the veranda with Halvorsen and Jonathan. Pointing, Halvorsen says, "There, to the north of that pond, is the Impenetrable Forest you're headed for. We've heard reports about a gorilla group up there, too."

"What's your theory why the gorillas are in the forest?" you ask.

"They're fleeing the villagers who graze their cattle in the park, as well as the poachers who hunt there," Halvorsen answers. "I don't have the manpower or the support of the local people to keep the park clear of either of them."

He points north again. "There's a special trail

from here to the Impenetrable Forest, which goes along the mountain slope. Jonathan and I could guide you. I'm curious about these reports myself. We could leave this morning."

You wonder for a moment what to do. You need an expert gorilla tracker like Mweri, and with any luck, he's waiting for you. But here's a chance to save precious time and start looking for the gorillas right away.

If you decide to say no to Halvorsen and stick to your plan to get Mweri now, turn to page 101.

If you decide to include Halvorsen and Jonathan and start from here, turn to page 13.

You drive up the dark road toward the Impenetrable Forest. Your headlights shine on a white sign: "Uganda Forestry Outpost, Impenetrable Forest District."

"We turn here," says Ed.

The road is now a one-lane track. It curves back and forth, following the contours of the steep volcanic mountains. It winds up, up, and the Land Rover's small engine labors in low gear.

Impatient, you peer ahead. Nothing to see but intense tropical darkness. Wait! There's a wink of light, like a candle, off to the left.

"Ed, look! What's that light? It's flickering in the forest, down there off the trail." As you near the light, it reflects off the branches of a tree overhead.

"Maybe it's a poacher camp!" you say. "Let's take it easy. Remember the roadblock we went through!"

Turn to page 109.

"Glad to have you two with us!" You shake hands with Halvorsen and Jonathan.

"I'll send someone for your tracker, Mweri. He should be able to track us from here if he's any good," says Halvorsen.

The four of you start up a forest trail. For hours the trail climbs up ridges and then sharply descends into ravines. It's tough going.

On the edge of a clearing, Halvorsen motions you over. He points at a round pile of crumpled leaves and branches in the center of a large shrub. The pile looks as if it's been woven.

"Gorilla nest!" you whisper.

"Yes, they make them every night to sleep in," he says. "Look, another." You all creep closer to the second nest. Suddenly Halvorsen freezes.

In another clearing ahead, a large dark head and shoulders poke above a bush. A gorilla! It moves into the open. Its upper shoulders, neck, and back are silver. It's a silverback; and silverbacks are usually the leaders of the gorilla groups they travel in. Several other adults move into sight, some with youngsters pulling at them and climbing on them. Ed counts nine: six adults, three babies. It's a complete group! Two babies climb into the midst of a large shrub and lounge there. One by one, they pick its purple blossoms and eat them, smacking their lips as if the food were candy.

"Rraaach!!" The silverback gives a shatteringly loud roar. He stares at the far side of the clearing. There's the third baby, and Jonathan's right next to it! What could he be doing?

Turn to page 28.

You pick up the gorillas' trail. After running along it for ten minutes, you hear the screams and wails of a young gorilla. Twenty feet ahead Jonathan sits on a lower branch of a large tree, holding a baby gorilla! Its mother is at the base of the tree, roaring in rage. She begins to climb up. Jonathan drops the baby. It scrambles to cling to its mother.

In silent menace the gorillas gather under Jonathan's tree!

"Help! Help!" he screams.

You take a chance. You burst from your hiding place, waving your arms and throwing sticks.

"Hoooo! Wraaa!" You scream and roar and head right for them. It works; they turn and run! You've saved Jonathan, but you're so furious that you can only glare at him and head back to your camp. Shaking with fear, Jonathan follows closely behind you.

Turn to page 105.

"I'm spooked by that leopard. Let's go back to the lean-to," you say.

Ed agrees. "Yes, let's get out of here. We've been through a lot!"

When you get to the lean-to, a man is cooking over a wood fire. His pack, made of animal skins, his canteen, and his machete sit by him on the ground.

You're relieved to see him. "Mweri! You found us!"

Before you can explain the delay in meeting him, he breaks in, saying, "I came through that mountain village near the forestry station. There's sickness there! I saw people lying on the ground vomiting. They had blue lips!"

You stand by his cook fire. "Mweri! Did you drink any water there? It sounds like cholera. That's a killer disease!"

"It does sound like cholera!" Ed says. "But there hasn't been any here for a long time. Well, if we need them, the medical clinic in Kisoro can give us anticholera shots."

You're worried about Mweri. Is it cholera? Did he get exposed to the disease in the village? What about your expedition?

If you decide to keep the expedition going, turn to page 33.

If you think you should all get the anticholera shots, turn to page 44.

"Let's follow them!" you say. "It'll be okay as long as we don't let them see us or get too close."

"Okay," Ed agrees. "As long as we're very careful not to frighten them. They're new to this territory, and they're nervous enough already."

As you walk on the narrow trail, Jonathan hangs back. And when the other two are well ahead of you, he says, "What do you think? One of those baby gorillas would make us lots of money! A guy from a European zoo came to see Halvorsen about getting a gorilla. Halvorsen got angry and said no. Help me catch one, and I'll split the money with you!"

"That's why you were watching that baby gorilla! No way, Jonathan! Are you crazy? You're a Gorilla Sanctuary employee!"

He drops the subject, saying, "I guess you're right. Let's forget it."

Both of you walk on in silence. You wonder if you can trust Jonathan now. Maybe it's all right, since he knows how you feel. But maybe you should bring the problem out in the open.

If you discuss your problem with Jonathan with the others, turn to page 25.

If you decide to trust him and see what happens, turn to page 39.

"Mweri!" you whisper. "What's that?"

He motions to you to keep quiet and follow. Now you see what the screaming was about. A baby gorilla is hanging by one of its feet from a fork in a spindly *Vernonia* tree! It's stuck, and its mother is holding it while she tries to pull its foot loose. She succeeds, and the baby jumps free of her.

You get your camera and note pad out and creep ahead to get a view. The baby is trying to stand on the silverback's stomach. The leader is lying on his back, propped up against the tree. You just have time to get some pictures before the mother runs over and scoops the baby up.

It's early afternoon, time for the group to rest after midday feeding. One of the mothers is building a nest by weaving together thin, pliable branches from a *Hypericum* tree. You quietly move uphill to get a better photograph of her.

A sound makes you look up. Staring down at you is a large, all-black gorilla. It's probably a male to judge from his size. Where did he come from? He's not part of the group below. He's a stranger!

With soft grunts, he moves downhill to you. What should you do? Running on this hill might be dangerous. Maybe you should remain motionless—but you can't guess what this gorilla will do. You could climb a tree, but can you outclimb a gorilla?

If you decide to run, turn to page 30.

If you remain motionless, turn to page 22.

If you climb a tree, turn to page 24.

"Ed, I'm going to get a rope and machete. Don't panic! I'll be back as soon as I can," you say.

A couple of hours later you make it back to the moss-covered rock with your tools. A leopard is crouched over the edge of the pit, poised ready to spring! Rays of sunlight shine on the animal; its dark spots glow in the bright light. For a moment you think, how beautiful! Then the leopard's tail twitches. It's about to leap.

"Yeoow!" you scream and heave the coil of rope at it. It snarls in fear and surprise. Then it spins around and slips into the bush without a noise.

"Am I glad to see you!" says Ed. "That leopard was getting bolder! I might have had company in a few more minutes!"

You tie the rope to a tree, pass an end down to Ed, and help him up over the edge.

"Ed, a leopard! I thought none were left in this part of Uganda," you say when he's out of the pit.

"They're rare here. They're endangered, too, like gorillas. People are taking up all their territory. They don't usually bother people—unless the people are trapped in a pit! They do hunt gorillas now and again. Bad luck that one's in the area!"

You're both tired, but it's only midday. It's tempting to go back to the lean-to for a rest. You wonder if Mweri is there, too. But you could use the time to continue Ed's circle plan. You don't want to let the gorillas get too far out of touch.

If you go back to the lean-to, turn to page 16.

If you continue to circle ahead of the gorillas, turn to page 40.

You're terribly frightened, but you stay right where you are. Perhaps it's the look in the gorilla's large brown eyes. He could just be curious. You wait. Slowly and deliberately, the gorilla walks toward you. You avoid staring into his eyes, and he

avoids staring into yours. He stops so close you can almost touch him!

His eyes seem kind. He does look curious! After a few moments, he slowly moves his head from side to side. By instinct you do the same. He stands up and reaches out to touch your face. You stay relaxed. He looks at you again and makes a soft grunting sound. Then he turns and moves uphill, away from you and the gorillas below. He disappears into the undergrowth.

You feel faint and weak in the knees; you're excited as you creep back to Ed and Mweri. What an encounter!

The End

Near you is a tree that looks easy to climb. You decide to play it safe, and minutes later you're at least twenty feet off the ground! Downhill you can see all nine gorillas in the silverback's group still taking their midday rest. Neither of your companions has spotted you.

With quick steps the strange gorilla moves to your tree, peers up at you with large brown eyes and, to your horror, begins to climb! He's big and heavy and has a hard time, but in a few minutes he's right below you.

You're afraid to yell down to your companions. Maybe it'll make the climbing gorilla attack! You're better off being quiet.

Your breath slows as his large shoulders push aside the branch below your feet. You hear him breathing. Moments pass, but neither of you moves. Then, impulsively, he reaches over and pulls on your bootlace!

You shriek. The cry alerts your companions below and sends the gorilla sliding down the tree trunk. For a speedy descent, he grips the trunk with his feet and lets his hands slide, like those of a fireman going down a pole! In a shower of bark, he hits the ground and runs off.

Ed and Mweri start laughing so loudly you can hear them up in your tree. You feel so silly and relieved, you start laughing yourself.

The End

You make up your mind to tell the others about Jonathan at your first rest stop.

All day the gorillas keep moving. Whenever you glimpse them, they disappear! As the day passes, you feel worried because the gorillas seem afraid.

When you stop for a rest and something to eat, Jonathan sits off by himself on a fallen tree.

"Jonathan spooked these gorillas. They sense he wants to steal a baby," you say to your companions.

Jonathan has heard you. He stops eating, and his face gets red. "Those gorillas are all going to end up dead, anyway! They're a dying breed. At least they'd have a chance in zoos!"

Halvorsen says, "What, Jonathan? Still thinking about stealing a baby for that zoo?" He turns to you. "What's going on here?"

You explain, "This morning he wanted to catch a baby for some zoo."

Halvorsen jumps up. "He's a park employee! That does it, Jonathan! You're fired!"

Turn to page 32.

"Yes, we've seen gorilla signs," the taller of the two hunters answers. "We can show them to you!"

The hunters take you south almost to the edge of the mountain forest. Farther south the lowland valley far below shows through the trees. You and Ed fall behind the others.

"*Wraagh!*" A silverback stands erect on the trail in front of the hunters! He roars again, beats his chest, and stops on the trail. He looks like the leader of the group you contacted before.

Before you can stop them, the hunters raise their spears!

Turn to page 50.

The youngster spots Jonathan, shrieks, and runs back to its mother, making little grunts. Jonathan retreats and rejoins your group.

"I wanted to get a better look!" he whispers.

You've been taking pictures. As Jonathan talks to you, the silverback spots your group and fixes Jonathan with a stare. With a fierce jerk he uproots a small bush and tosses it up in the air. He charges toward you twice, stopping each time after a few feet. Whirling around, he grunts to the other gorillas. They move past him. He follows, and they vanish into the forest.

What was Jonathan up to? you wonder. No time to figure it out now. Should you follow the gorillas or let them get over their scare?

If you leave the gorillas alone to get over their scare, turn to page 36.

If you follow the gorillas right now, turn to page 17.

You look around for a dead branch to help Ed out of the pit. There's one nearby. Handing it into the pit, you say, "Careful, Ed. Go easy on it! It's pretty thin!"

You reach down and grab Ed's hand. He's almost out! Then—*snap*! The branch breaks. Before you can let go, you've fallen into the pit with Ed!

Ed helps you to stand. Luckily you're okay. Neither of you says anything. You both know you may die.

Hours pass. Mosquitoes swarm around you. You're beginning to need water.

A rustle above your head startles you. Two men lean over the edge and peer down. "Hey, we don't catch people, just antelopes! Sorry!" one says.

Using a pole they cut from a nearby sapling, they help you out. Both are tall men, and each carries a spear and a machete.

"Thanks for getting us out," Ed says to them.

"What are you doing in the forest?" the taller hunter asks.

Should you tell them? Maybe they could help you. They know the forest. But they *are* hunters. Maybe they'll harm the gorillas if they learn about them.

If you say, "We're looking for gorillas. Have you seen any signs of them?" *turn to page 27.*

If you say, "That's not important. We're glad you came along and helped us. Goodbye," *turn to page 38.*

Run for it! The huge black gorilla keeps on coming. He's so close you can see the shiny black hair on his chest glistening in the sun.

You whirl around. There's a trail off to the right, and you bolt for it, away from the gorilla and your companions. You dash downhill along an indistinct track. A branch whips across your face. Your eyes fill with tears; you can't see. You take a few more steps—and you're falling! *Crack!* Pain shoots through your left leg.

You're in a long, rectangular pit. It looks man-made; sawdust covers the bottom. Your leg hurts too much to move. There's nothing to do except remain still and wait for your companions.

Minutes later Mweri and Ed lean over the edge. They lift you to safety and put your leg in a splint. You fell into a saw pit, a deep trench used to saw logs into planks. Your expedition is over.

The End

Halvorsen motions to Jonathan. "Let's go. We're going back!" He turns to you and Ed. "Sorry! Good luck getting pictures and a story on the gorillas. At least we've found them here in the Impenetrable Forest. If your tracker shows up at park headquarters, I'll tell him where to find you."

After they leave, you and Ed build a thatched roof lean-to for a camp so that you don't have to keep returning to the park. You camp for the night.

Next morning Ed suggests, "Let's circle away from the gorillas and let them move alone for a while. If we keep tracking them, they may flee from their new territory."

"Okay," you say. "Let's go!"

Ed leads. He's following an antelope track. He walks around a moss-covered rock. Moments later you hear, "Help!" and a crash of breaking branches. He has fallen into a hunter's antelope trap!

"I'm not hurt," Ed calls up to you. "I just feel foolish. I should have watched where I was going."

There's no way for Ed to get out; you can't reach him because the pit is too deep.

It's risky to leave Ed helpless, but your tools and rope are back at the lean-to. If you stay and look around, maybe you'll be able to find a branch strong enough for him to climb out on.

If you go back to the lean-to for tools,
turn to page 20.

If you try to find a branch to get Ed out,
turn to page 29.

You decide to keep going. Ed said there hasn't been any cholera around for a long time, so Mweri can't possibly have it.

"Let's eat and turn in for the night. If you feel all right in the morning, Mweri, we can find those gorillas Jonathan frightened," you say.

The next morning Mweri feels fine. By noon he has circled to the southern area of the Impenetrable Forest and picked up the gorillas' path. You are hiding, getting ready to take some photos without letting the gorillas see you. They're still frightened by their contact with Jonathan.

"See, they did keep moving, right to the edge of the forest!" Ed whispers.

"Yes, they're the same group," you answer. "See that baby Jonathan frightened? I'm getting some good shots of it. It hasn't learned! Look, it's wandering away from its mother again!"

Turn to page 42.

You walk into the center of the meadow to see the dead animals. Maybe poachers did it! As you peer through the haze, you see the bodies of several predators—a hyena, a leopard. Near the half-rotted body of a deer, two vultures lie crumpled!

Maybe the strange mist is poisonous! You sniff. There's no smell. You feel great! You're alert, and something about this mysterious meadow gives you a good feeling. The grass is so green! The dead animals don't bother you. You walk into the center to examine a tiny animal.

You crouch down to get a better look. Wow! Do

you feel good! You laugh out loud and decide to show this place to Ed and Mweri.

You don't know it but you've found a *matsuko* meadow. The mist is carbon dioxide gas. It's seeping out of the ground from the volcano nearby. First it makes you happy, then drowsy. If you fall asleep in a *matsuko* meadow, you never wake up.

You sit down for a moment to enjoy all these wonderful feelings! You forget what you wanted to do. That's all right; it doesn't matter anymore. You lie down.

The End

"Best we leave them alone for a day," you say. "They've had a bad scare, and gorillas like their privacy, you know. We've made contact with them. We'll pick up their trail from here tomorrow."

"Well," Halvorsen says, "too bad. Jonathan and I should get back to the park, then."

"We'll come with you. Maybe Mweri will show up, if your messenger found him," you say.

Back at park headquarters late that afternoon, Mweri does arrive.

You greet him and apologize for all the confusion. "But we've had some beginner's luck," you explain. "We spotted a group today! We

spooked them, though. Tomorrow we'll try to make contact again."

You, Ed, and Mweri start out early the next morning. After tracking the gorillas into an area that's quite level, Mweri stops and points. "Here's where they felt safe again and slowed down. See all those separate trails they've made? It's where they began exploring for things to eat."

"How far ahead are they now?" Ed asks.

"They're close!" Mweri answers. "From now on, crouch low and keep quiet. It won't be long!"

Crouching down, you follow Mweri through a thick tunnel of vegetation. The going is tough. The gorilla trail is right through a bunch of nettles that sting your face and hands no matter how careful you are.

"Aieee! Aieee!" Shrieks that sound like those of a human baby come from ahead on the left!

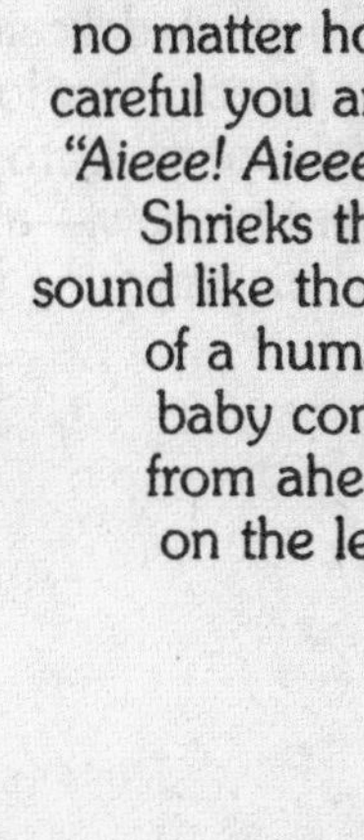

Turn to page 19.

After you say goodbye to them, the two hunters turn to their antelope trap. You and Ed continue along the trail.

You're lucky! The sunny weather holds. After you've skirted the shoulder of a mountain, you find a trail heading south, the direction the gorillas seem to have taken. It passes through some bamboo trees, then leads to an old overgrown slope.

"Careful!" Ed warns. "Let's move quietly! They're close—look! Here's where they built a few nests to rest today. They must have been eating bamboo shoots back there!"

You both creep forward on all fours. You see the gorillas at the bottom of the slope, several hundred yards away.

"Ed, I wonder if that's the same group . . ."

Snap! A delicate, dry, breaking sound makes you freeze. You look back.

A leopard! It crouches on the trail behind you. It begins to growl—an incredibly low, smooth sound. And it's watching you, not the gorillas!

Turn to page 48.

You decide to trust Jonathan for now. For two days the gorillas elude you as they move through the forest. They are easy to follow, though, because they leave a clear trail of broken plants and chewed stalks. But they're moving faster than you or Ed remembers them moving from your previous field studies. They keep just out of your sight. There's no way to make contact with them or even to see them. You make camp each night in the forest.

"I'm worried," Ed says. "They're heading for the southern edge of the forest. We're frightening them." After a discussion the four of you decide to spend the next day in camp to let the gorillas settle down. Maybe they'll stop running away if you stop pursuing them.

That afternoon Jonathan is gone. Maybe he's after the gorillas on his own!

Turn to page 14.

"Let's keep circling south to see what's happened to our gorillas," you say.

"Fine. I'm worried that that leopard might be on their trail. Let's go!" Ed replies.

First you climb around a volcanic mountain. Giant groundsel and *Lobelia* plants, taller than a person, dot the rocky slope. The giant groundsels have sunburst-shaped displays of pointed leaves at the top of thick, shaggy trunks. The *Lobelia* look like giant cactus plants.

Thousands of feet down the mountain is a strip of meadow. Around it are *Hagenia* trees hung with great drapes of Spanish moss.

"This is good gorilla territory, Ed! Look at all those *Hagenia* trees," you say.

Minutes later Ed finds a fresh gorilla track. You both smell the familiar traces of fresh gorilla dung.

"They're near here!" he whispers. You both crawl forward.

You spot a couple of gorillas! They're eating celery stalks in a clearing off the meadow. You grab your camera.

"Look, it's the same group! There's the baby gorilla Jonathan scared. See, it's up to its old trick! It's wandered far away from its mother and the others," you say.

Through the telephoto lens, you spot the leopard before Ed does. It's stalking the baby!

"Ed—!" you start to say, but suddenly the leopard springs and clutches the gorilla!

"Aieeee! Aieeee!" the baby screams. It struggles away before the leopard can bite it and cowers in a small bush.

"Look, it's the same leopard that trapped you," you say. "Part of its tail is missing!"

In seconds the leopard will spring again! Maybe you should try to scare it away. But the adults are running toward the baby's screams, and they're getting close.

If you decide to try to frighten the leopard away from the baby gorilla, turn to page 43.

If you decide to stay hidden because the gorillas are coming, turn to page 62.

The sun is still shining, which is unusual for these high mountains where rain and mist usually sweep in during the late morning. Rays of sunlight shine on the baby as he climbs a *Vernonia* sapling. Hanging by his feet from a thin branch, he tests its strength by jerking up and down violently. With his arms flailing the air, he looks like a crazy upside-down bird trying to fly!

Crack! Down he goes, shrieking in alarm, still holding on to the broken-off branch! He rushes to his mother for comfort.

You try to keep from laughing so your camera won't jiggle when you shoot.

Back in camp later that afternoon, Mweri starts to vomit.

"I feel weak!" Mweri says. "I did drink some water in that village! It didn't make sense when you asked yesterday. Is that how you get cholera?"

"That's why I asked!" you answer. "Mweri, we'll get you to Kisoro to that clinic right away."

"I'll take him," Ed says quietly.

You wonder about it. You trust Ed to take care of Mweri, but you're responsible for him. One of you does need to stay in contact with the gorillas.

If you take Mweri back yourself,
turn to page 56.

If you ask Ed to take Mweri back,
turn to page 54.

"Yaaah! Hey!" First you, then Ed stands up and starts yelling. Ed throws a stick; it crashes in front of the leopard, startling it! Hooting and screaming, two gorillas run to the baby.

"*Wraaagh!*" The silverback roars and charges at the confused leopard. It snarls at him and hesitates with one paw up; its tail lashes the vegetation. Suddenly it turns and vanishes!

The silverback pounds through the underbrush after it, roaring. The *thwack thwack* of its chest beats echo in the forest.

"Yahoo! Hope the baby is okay, Ed!" you say.

Its mother has scooped it up and is licking the claw marks. The baby clings to her and stops wailing.

"That leopard's probably not going to risk another encounter with that silverback! He'll be on guard. Maybe the gorillas will stay—this is good territory for them. But they've had a bad scare," Ed says as you hike back to the lean-to.

The gorilla group does stay! And using the lean-to as a base, you establish contact with them and visit them almost daily. Your photographs and story in *African Naturalist* help Halvorsen raise money to establish a preserve for the gorillas in the Impenetrable Forest.

The End

"Mweri, Ed, we'll all head back to Kisoro for cholera shots. I hear the shots don't always work, but they sure can help! We've got enough light to get to the Land Rover."

While you're getting your shots in the clinic, the director comes in.

"Gentlemen, we've just found out there has been an outbreak of cholera in that village! Five cases and two deaths already! I think you'll be fine, but I'm going to have to keep you in Kisoro in quarantine for a couple of weeks."

Your expedition is over! While you're all in quarantine, you've got lots of time on your hands. One evening Mweri and Ed pretend they're gorillas. You start snapping pictures. Mweri gets his silver-colored antelope skin and drapes it on his back. He makes a great silverback.

"Wraagh!" In the corner of the room, he crouches, then stands, faces you, and beats his chest.

At least you'll have *some* gorilla pictures to take back with you. Maybe *African Naturalist* needs a humor section.

The End

"Where are these gorilla hunters?" you ask the first poacher.

"We saw their camp at the edge of a clearing down there," he says and points to a spot in the bamboo back down the path. "There's a trail nearby." Then the two deer poachers vanish into the thick vegetation at the side of the trail.

"I think he means that saddle area between this mountain and the next," Ed says.

But Mweri is worried. "Those deer poachers are not from my tribe. I don't trust them!" he tells you and Ed.

You take over and lead the way out of the bamboo forest. In the saddle area the vegetation is thick. Ed and Mweri help clear a path with their machetes. Then you find the trail the poachers mentioned. "Water buffalo and elephants use this trail to cross here. Look at their marks," says Ed.

"Be careful! Poachers sometimes set those trip-log traps for water buffalo along here," Mweri warns.

Turn to page 63.

"Wait!" you say, standing up. "We're following those gorillas. They haven't hurt your daughter!"

"We saw gorillas in the bamboo forest yesterday," the child's father says. "We've never seen them before, and they scared us! We heard strange screams from the forest this morning, and now my little daughter is missing. Will you help us find her?"

You think for a moment. You're sure the gorillas haven't hurt this man's daughter, and they'll probably find her soon. You want to stay near the gorillas you've just found. But if these men don't find the girl soon, they may harm the gorillas or get hurt themselves.

If you decide to help the men find the girl, turn to page 78.

If you decide to stay in your camp, turn to page 73.

You dart past Ed along the trail and try to run for it.

Something smashes into you from behind! You smell the rich moist earth as your face hits the ground.

The leopard closes its jaws on the spot where your neck and right shoulder meet.

The End

Just as Ed says, "Hey, wait, put your spears down!" the gorilla charges. The first hunter launches his spear, palm up and open.

The light spear cuts the gorilla's side. Enraged, the gorilla attacks the first hunter. Blood spurts from a deep laceration on his thigh. Then the gorilla disappears into the bush. From a distance come the sounds of gorilla hoots; then the sounds fade.

You and Ed help the wounded hunter. With leaves, moss, and vines the other hunter makes a field dressing for his companion's torn thigh.

The hunters spread word of the gorilla attack through the villages around the Impenetrable Forest. The Parks and Game Department forbids your expedition to continue.

The End

"Hey, Ed, Mweri! Wake up! Come over here!" you call from the meadow's edge.

Ed shows up, rubbing his eyes. "What do you want?"

"Look at this place! It's so quiet; the grass is so green! And look at all these dead animals, Ed!" you say and grab his arm.

"That's a *matsuko* meadow!" says Ed, completely awake now. "See that haze in the middle? It's carbon dioxide gas. It's deadly in that concentration! It comes from volcanic disturbances underground. Look at that grass! It makes plants grow beautifully!"

"Good thing I didn't go out there!" you say. "It might have killed me, too! Let's get out of here and camp somewhere else!"

Next day Mweri picks up the gorillas' trail near where he spotted their night nests two days before. It's an area of *Hypericum* trees, and the gorillas shaped their soft, pliable branches to build their sleeping nests. There are seven of the nests, shaped like crude bathtubs.

The trail goes along the edge of a shallow, flat-bottomed ravine. Mweri points down into the ravine. "Another *matsuko* meadow!" he says.

"What if the gorillas wandered into it?" you say. "Let's have a look."

Turn to page 70.

To make a shelter from the rain you take a poncho from your pack and snap it to the one

you're wearing. You drape the joined ponchos over a limb from a fallen tree. They'll make a crude, open-ended tent as soon as you spread out the lower edges and tie them to plants.

The cold makes you stiff and clumsy. You accidentally knock a dead branch off the tree with a loud crash. That does it! Those gorillas must be a mile away by now! But at least your tent is rigged. You sit down in it and peer through the rain.

The gorillas are still there! In fact, they've left their shelter to stare in *your* direction. They're fascinated by your struggle! You start to take pictures. Then you hear something.

"Hey, Bill, where are we?"

Crash! "Oh, this awful jungle!"

"Aie! Aie! Aiii!!" The gorillas scream in alarm at the voices and run toward the mountain. Their silverback pauses, gives an ear-shattering roar in the direction of the disturbance, and vanishes after his family.

You climb a tree and spot five people in a clearing. They've got what looks like a movie camera and lots of heavy equipment. It must be a movie crew.

With a groan, you climb down. The rain is letting up. You wonder if you should talk to this bunch and try to keep them from scaring the gorillas or if you should follow the gorillas now that they've begun to accept you.

If you try to talk to the movie crew, turn to page 98.

If you stay with the gorillas, turn to page 80.

You watch Ed support Mweri as they walk slowly out of camp. "Good luck!" you shout.

Then clouds swarm over the sun. It's going to rain after all! The rain's just late.

The fire you've lit cheers you. First drizzle, then rain rustles the thatched roof of the lean-to you and Ed made. It's getting dark—time to cook something to eat.

But you don't feel hungry. Your stomach rolls and churns. You must be getting sick, too!

"Wonder if I'll have the strength to walk out of here tomorrow to find help," you say to the fire.

All night you continue to be sick. The night is endless as the rain continues.

You're too weak to bother with the fire. It goes out. For a while you have a little peace. But you're thirsty. You grab the canteen and drink.

Wait! It's Mweri's canteen! You drank some of his water the day before when you were watching the gorillas. That's what made you sick! He probably filled his canteen at that village!

It sure seems like cholera. You're getting more and more dehydrated, and you scream with pain from cramps in your legs and stomach.

Daylight heartens you. At last the rain stops. You try to walk. You can't, so you have to crawl. It's so slow! You stop to rest and curl up to ease your cramping muscles. Your arms look so thin and blue, you think vaguely as you cup your head in them. You feel more tired than you've ever felt.

All you can do now is lie still and wait. You hope Ed will find you before it's too late.

The End

You can't understand what the voices are saying, and in a few moments the sounds fade away. You're furious at the disturbance because the gorillas have fled. Just when they were beginning to get used to you!

It's easy to follow the gorillas' trail uphill. They've moved single file and smashed down the leafy undergrowth and vines in a clear path. The trail goes past a clearing with an unused lean-to in it. It's a good place to camp for the night. The gorillas will build sleeping nests nearby. In the morning, if you're lucky, you'll have a chance to contact them again.

The night is cold, and your sleeping bag is wet from the rain. You can't sleep much so you just wait for the dawn. Luck is with you! When the sun rises, you carefully follow their trail and find the gorillas still in their night nests.

Turn to page 59.

Gently you lead Mweri to the Land Rover. It's hard for him. He is so weak you have to hold him up. His lips are blue, and his skin is loose and clammy. He looks small and old.

On the drive to Kisoro, rain begins to fall as night comes. The red dirt road turns muddy. You have to keep stopping to wipe the mud off the headlights.

"Good luck, Mweri!" you say when you finally reach the clinic. "We'll be back soon! I'm heading

back to park headquarters for the night before the road washes out."

It's pouring. The rain makes it hard to see, and the mud has become worse. The driving is slow; you stop to put the Land Rover in four-wheel drive. A couple of minutes later you're forced to stop. A stream has flooded the road!

You inch the Land Rover forward into the swirling red-brown water. Suddenly headlights appear on the other side! Should you wait and try to get help from the oncoming vehicle or try to make it yourself? If you wait, maybe you won't make it!

If you decide to wait for help, stop the Land Rover and turn to page 100.

If you try to make it yourself, keep moving and turn to page 75.

You plan to spend the morning watching the gorillas and taking pictures. The sun glints on the dew that covers their thick black fur. They lazily reach out of their nests for a tasty snack, breakfast in bed! They yawn and stretch, and one by one leave their nests to begin morning eating. To keep them in sight, you crawl quietly on all fours. You pretend to eat the wild celery they're busy picking, stripping of its outer layers, and eating. They spot you, of course, and the silverback stares at you for a long time. You remain on all fours, and soon they go back to eating. They're accepting you!

Around noon the silverback stops moving and eating, and the group rests. You stop where the group can see you. They pay no attention to you.

All of them rest and nap except the playful baby, which plays closer and closer to you. You take one close-up shot after another as the youngster impishly peers right into your camera inches from the lens. Then it reaches for your camera!

If you let the youngster take your camera, turn to page 85.

If you hold on to your camera, turn to page 99.

You spot a thick tree branch hanging over the trail. It's just the right height for you! You grab the branch and swing up.

Whish! The wind from the charging buffalo moves the leaves on your branch. That was close!

Snorting in rage, the buffalo catches the child's father on one of her horns. He flies off into the air, landing in a bush. That saves his life. For a moment the water buffalo paws at the bush, but the man is out of reach. With a last snort, the beast turns and disappears into the forest.

Turn to page 66.

You remain quiet and stay hidden with Ed.

The leopard tenses in a crouch, ready to spring. The large muscle on its right rear leg trembles beneath the fur.

"*Wraaagh!*" The silverback spots the leopard and charges as two other gorillas run to the baby in the bush.

The leopard lunges at the silverback. But the male gorilla is ready. He grapples with the leopard briefly, lifts it in his huge arms, and bites it in the back of the neck.

The leopard screams and lashes out with its powerful hind feet. *Rippp!* Its claws dig deep into the silverback's stomach. He drops the leopard with a howl. Blood oozes between his hands as he holds his stomach in surprise and pain.

The leopard drags itself away. Bellowing, the silverback calls to his group and disappears with them. Crashing sounds from the forest get fainter as the gorillas flee.

Next day Mweri finds you at the lean-to. He helps you track the gorillas to the western edge of the Impenetrable Forest where it borders on Zaire. In Zaire they disappear. You dare not follow; recent border conflicts between Zaire and Uganda make it too dangerous. You hope the gorillas are safe.

The End

You're nervous, and it makes you supercareful. Your eyes dart back and forth across the path, looking for the tiny pegs that hold the nearly invisible trip wire. An animal only has to brush the trip wire, and a log weighing hundreds of pounds with a long knife fixed in it will come smashing down.

The trail narrows; lots of vegetation hangs over it. The light is dim. You slow down and walk bent over so as not to miss any wire. Wait, that looks like one!

Your heart beats faster with dread and excitement. You motion the others to wait. You kneel to examine the wire and the little pegs that hold it in place. But as you push away the bush above it, you hit a second trip wire!

You only have time to pull back a bit as the giant log above you is silently released and crashes down.

Turn to page 65.

64

Crack! The impact flings you onto the trail—right on top of the other trip wire! A second log crashes down and the blade stuck in it drives into your back.

The End

"That was close!" he says after you and the others help him up. "But I'm all right, just banged up! We're not far from my village."

In the village the child's mother shows you and Mweri where she last saw her daughter playing that morning.

"She was helping me weed this vegetable patch. I went away to get some water, and she was gone when I came back!" she says.

Mweri walks slowly around the edge of the vegetable patch and that of the forest. He stops to peer at a bent leaf and then examines a faint impression in the earth under it. "Here," he says.

The trail leads far from the village. Beside some thick, vine-covered bushes, Mweri stops to look for the next trail clue.

Then you all hear crying! It sounds like a child, and it's coming from the other side of the bushes and vines!

Turn to page 89.

The forest is quiet. The three of you crouch down on a trail and peer ahead for signs of gorilla movement. As you rise, you tell Mweri, "They must still be ahead of us—"

Suddenly sharp screams burst from the thick vegetation to the left of the trail ahead.

"Gorillas!" Mweri whispers. "They saw you and gave the alarm!"

Farther away high-pitched calls repeat over and over. In the top of a tree ahead, three black balls of fur bounce from branch to branch and start sliding down a thick vine to the ground. Gorilla babies!

"Those are their mothers calling them!" Ed says.

The last baby down the vine jumps on the shoulders of the one under it, and they wrestle for a second. Then they all scamper off toward their mothers' calls.

"Let's keep after them, Mweri!" you say excitedly. "It's true! Gorillas *have* migrated to the Impenetrable Forest!"

"They're scared now. If we keep tracking them, they may flee from this forest! It'll be easy to contact them again tomorrow. Let them get used to us gradually," Mweri advises you.

It's tempting to stay on the trail of the gorillas. You've waited so long to find them and get started on your article. But perhaps waiting for a day will pay off later.

If you keep following the gorillas, turn to page 71.

If you wait until tomorrow to contact the gorillas, turn to page 77.

It has to be the baby gorilla! Little sobs mix with the wailing. You walk quietly toward the sound, stopping every few steps to listen and look.

Then you see it. Hanging from a tree branch is a cage made of split bamboo and vines. Inside, a female baby gorilla shrinks away from the sight of you. Last night all the noise probably frightened her so much she didn't dare cry out loud.

The baby gorilla is in pitiful shape. She looks half starved, and she's sick. She cowers on the bottom of her cage. Her wrists have nasty cuts, perhaps from her capture.

You decide to carry the baby gorilla to the outpost and try to nurse her back to health. You name her Surprise. Every day you feed her fresh assorted vines, berries, and leaves. Thanks to your attention and love, Surprise lives. Soon she accepts you and clings to you as if you were her mother.

Then Ed returns. "Those gorilla poachers are in jail," he says as he greets you. "The two who helped us got off with a warning."

Surprise jumps out from behind a chair and clings to you. She's scared of Ed!

"Hey! Look! You found the baby!" Ed exclaims.

Turn to page 117.

The meadow glows like an emerald in the dark surrounding forest. A soft haze of carbon dioxide hangs over it.

Holding your breath, you approach this new *matsuko* meadow.

"No! Not gorillas!" You're the first one there, and first to see the black lumps lying peacefully near the center of the deadly clearing. "No!"

"I count nine," says Ed. "Must be a whole group. There's the leader, the silverback, there. Those must be mothers, the ones holding the babies."

All you can do is take photographs with a telephoto lens. At least they died together and peacefully. The images in the viewfinder look so relaxed. The gorillas appear to be asleep in the mist.

The End

"Let's keep following the gorillas, Mweri," you say. "We'll have to make sure we don't scare them."

Mweri takes a circular route, trying not to frighten the gorillas. Fog moves in, and it begins to rain. The forest is cold and wet.

Mweri pauses by a large outcropping of rock on the ridge he's been following. He points down. "There are the gorillas again, feeding just off that clearing. I think we can sneak down without letting them hear us if we're careful."

He's right, and you forget how cold you are. There are the three gorilla babies, and this time their mothers are visible. One of them is under a leaning tree, weaving branches from a tree into a circle. She's making a nest. The leaning trunk shelters her from the rain. Her baby is trying to make a nest, too, right out in the open.

"Okay, we've contacted the group," you whisper to Ed and Mweri. "Let's go back to the outpost and dry off! It should be easy to contact them again near this same spot tomorrow morning."

Turn to page 76.

"Can I help you?" you ask.

The tall, bearded man smiles and says, "Yes! We're lost. Our tracker quit this morning. Will you help us get some footage?"

You agree and silently guide them to the trail the gorillas made as they fled. You crouch down on all fours, and the crew imitates you.

"They may be around still," you whisper.

"You mean they just came this way?" asks the youngest crew member. "Oh, boy!" He drops his pack and runs up the trail of crushed undergrowth.

Furious, you catch up to him and try to pull him into a crouch. "Better not push it—"

A deafening roar splits the quiet. The young man screams and runs back along the gorilla track. A black gorilla bursts from the undergrowth after him, hitting him from behind. They roll out of sight.

"Help!" the man screams from the underbrush. The black gorilla bolts into the vegetation and disappears. It's probably one of the young males from the group. He must have stayed behind to protect the rear of his group, become frightened, and charged the young man.

Disgusted, you help him up. "Oooh, my arm! I think I broke it," he sobs.

You lead him and the rest of the crew back to the forestry outpost camp. They've had enough. In a few minutes they leave for the nearest town.

Discouraged, you search for the gorilla group for days. At last you have to admit defeat. They've vanished! Bad luck for you and *African Naturalist*!

The End

You tell the villagers that you are going to stay in your camp. "We watched the gorillas all morning, and they were calm; no sign of your daughter," you say. "But we'll keep watch for her! Good luck!"

The two villagers leave. The rain stops half an hour later.

"Listen!" says Mweri.

The distant sounds of chanting and drums float up from the edge of the forest.

"They're getting their courage up for a gorilla hunt!" Ed says.

"Let's see if we can herd the gorillas away from here before the villagers get to them!" you say.

Mweri picks up the gorilla trail where you had broken off contact with them earlier in the day. In a grove of tall *Hypericum* trees he bends down. "They're near! Smell that? It's gorilla dung. See, they were eating that plant with the red flowers that grows in those trees."

Just as you spread out to try to drive the gorillas away from danger, a murmuring sound, then a low hooting begins!

"Hoo! Hoo! Hoo!" It's ahead, up the trail. Then it comes from behind. *"Hoo! Hoo!"* Now it comes from both sides of the trail. The hoots change to barking sounds. They cease. No wind rustles a leaf, no bird calls. It's eerie!

Turn to page 84.

It works! The man and the woman imitate your movements and manage to film scenes of the gorillas eating and building midday nests to rest in. You get clear shots of the gorilla babies climbing trees and playing with one another and with the adults.

By the last day of filming, the gorillas pay little attention to the three of you. The cameraman is tracking two adults. They wander from tree to tree, searching for just the best-tasting vine leaves. Two youngsters follow them around.

"Look!" you whisper to him. "Get that youngster. It's watching you and your camera."

The youngster is staring right at the movie camera. With a hop, it leaves the others, runs within five feet of the camera, does a back flip, and runs away! You photograph the cameraman and the youngster with your own camera.

Success! Your article and photos in *African Naturalist* help Halvorsen and other officials protect the gorillas in the Impenetrable Forest.

The End

You keep moving into the swirling water. If you wait, you may not make it at all!

The water rises to the tops of your wheels at just about the midpoint of the flood; your headlights begin picking up the road on the other side.

Slish! The Land Rover noses down and settles deep in the water! The flooding stream has eaten a deep hole into the road. You've driven into six feet of fast-moving water!

Cold, gritty water fills the Land Rover in seconds. Its coldness shocks you, and you can't suck in much breath from up near the roof!

Turn to page 118.

A week passes, and you've had success staying in contact. It's too far to go back and forth to the outpost each day, so you've built a lean-to shelter in the forest area the gorillas occupy. Already the gorillas don't pay much attention to you when you contact them each morning.

"They don't mind us as long as we crouch over and pretend to eat what they like to eat, like this wild celery," Ed says. You're close to the two young adult males that often seem to guard the group's back trail. You start taking photos.

"Hoo, hoo, hoo, hoo, hoo!" A rapid series of hoots comes from a gorilla behind you.

Ten feet from where you crouch in the wild celery, a massive silvery head thrusts out of the thick vegetation.

"Look! Another silverback!" you whisper. "I've never seen him. He's not part of this group! Where'd he come from?"

Turn to page 93.

"Okay, we'll wait till tomorrow, Mweri," you say. "We've got plenty to do now that we've located gorillas. Let's set up our camp here, near them!"

"I saw a good camping place near that ridge we came over," says Ed. "There's a stream for water."

It starts raining, which is common in these high mountains. It's cold, too, and cutting saplings for the lean-to is mean work. When it's finished, Mweri builds a fire. You dry your clothes by it and try to warm up.

The rain continues, and the gray afternoon light is dim, the color of smoke from the fire.

Suddenly the calm is broken. Two men burst into the campsite and run up to you. "My three-year-old daughter is missing!" one of them shouts. "We think gorillas have killed her!"

Turn to page 47.

"Let's get going. Show us where the little girl was last seen," you say. "Mweri, your tracking skill is going to be useful now!"

The father guides you along the trail to his village. The rain has soaked the red earth, and it's like grease underfoot.

"Watch it!" he yells. "Water buffalo with her calf up there! We've made her angry. Run!" A huge water buffalo stands right in the middle of the trail! Rain glistens on her wicked-looking, thick, curved horns.

Quick! It's charging. You've got to decide what to do!

If you run, turn to page 116.

If you leap for a tree branch and climb, turn to page 60.

Deciding to stay with the gorillas, you climb down from the tree and sneak away from the noisy film crew. You follow the gorillas until late in the afternoon. They stay ahead of you, moving toward the lower slopes of the mountain, away from the area where you discovered them. You break off tracking them and return to your camp at the forestry outpost for the night.

The next day you recontact the gorillas. You sit under a tree and watch two of them. Their dark heads and shoulders poke above the vegetation.

As you try to figure out what plants they are eating, you hear a voice call, "Bill! Bill! Come look at these big nests. Maybe gorillas stayed here last night." Their voices carry through the forest from a great distance.

The strange sounds startle the two gorillas. Their leader calls and the two you're watching disappear after him.

The film crew never finds them, but the noise and commotion they make drives the gorillas higher and higher up the mountain.

They keep moving. You camp out for the night so you can be near them. The next day they're harder to track through the thinning vegetation and cinders high up on the old volcano.

The third day you search for traces of their path. You've lost it! Maybe they've headed back to the Gorilla Sanctuary Park in their fright. Maybe poachers have trapped or shot them! They've left the Impenetrable Forest, and you have no story for *African Naturalist.*

The End

You decide to scare the silverback away to help protect the mountain gorillas. "Ed, you circle to the right; Mweri, take the left. I'll head right for him. We'll drive him ahead of us. Make lots of noise! Be careful!"

In a sweeping arc, you all move out, shouting and roaring. Off to the side, Ed and Mweri yell and throw sticks. It works! The silverback crashes ahead of you.

An hour later you've driven the silverback a couple of miles from the gorilla group.

"That should do it!" you call out to Ed and Mweri. "Let's head home to the lean-to for the night."

Next day you're lucky. Right away Mweri picks up the trail of the group from the spot where the fight took place. Tufts of black hair and mashed-down vegetation mark the starting point.

The group recognizes you and greets you with soft rumbling sounds when you reach them a few minutes later. You get to work photographing the baby gorillas. They're right out in the open.

One of them creeps toward you. It's following something on the ground. The baby reaches out a hand, then jumps back. The same thing happens again! Through the telephoto lens you see what it is: a frog! The baby catches it.

You get a good shot of it holding the frog inches from its face as it puzzles over the creature.

"*Wraagh!*" Its mother bellows from somewhere near. That's the danger call!

Turn to page 96.

You look their leader in the eyes. "Will you help me?" you ask.

He pauses and says, "Well, we're stuck here, anyway. How can we help you?"

You reply quickly, "Look, I'd like to make a deal with you. You've got as much right as I do to study these gorillas. If you cooperate with me and keep quiet, I'll help you film them."

The leader agrees, and you take the crew back to camp, explaining that the gorillas need to rest and calm down.

The next day two of them, a cameraman and a woman with a tape recorder and a special outdoor microphone, come with you and make contact with the gorilla group. You ask the two to sit quietly and not use their equipment until the gorillas get used to their presence.

The following day you and the film crew make contact with the gorilla group again.

"I think they're used to us," you whisper. "Try shooting. Don't stand up!"

Turn to page 74.

For a few moments you gaze after the gorillas, in a trance.

"We'll have a hard time tracking them in this fog," Ed says, breaking your trance.

"What are they doing heading to the top of the volcano?" you ask. "Let's try to find them!"

You have to give up. The fog is thick, and the gorillas leave no trail on the bare rock.

The search is fruitless. The gorillas have disappeared, and you call the expedition off several days later.

"I don't understand why they went so far from their usual territory. What were they after? Nothing to eat up here," Ed says and peers into the clouds that swirl around the rim of the old volcano's crater.

"Maybe they were desperate to find a safe place. I don't know. That's the way expeditions end sometimes," you say.

You can never forget the look in the eyes of the gorilla you met that day in the mist.

The End

"They're all around us!" you say. You huddle together and look at one another.

"I don't remember gorillas acting like this!" Ed says.

"Let's get out of here!" Mweri mutters.

Back at camp you feel calmer in the shelter of your lean-to.

"Listen! The gorillas have followed us!" says Mweri. At first you can't hear anything. Then it comes, a low murmuring sound, like hundreds of voices saying prayers. It comes from three sides of the camp! It's not loud, but it is menacing.

"Quick! Let's move!" you say. Grabbing your packs, you all head away from the sound. Behind you and to both sides, the gorillas' hoots and barking calls keep pace.

"Mweri, they're herding *us*! What direction are we going?" you ask.

"South. We're going to end up on the road east of the outpost we started from!" he says.

"That's it! We're just about there," Ed says and points through the near trees. Far down in a valley of terraced garden plots winds the familiar-looking road.

You all relax. It's safe. The normal bird and insect sounds of the forest surround you again. The gorillas have driven you away from their new home.

The End

You smile and relax your grip on the camera. You're sure you can trust this friendly little animal. Gently the young gorilla handles the camera. It peers into the lens shyly and holds the camera up in the air. It looks at you, then at the camera. It holds the camera up to its face and points it at you! You laugh at the sight and wonder if you look just as silly pointing the camera at the gorillas.

The youngster puts your camera down near you and scampers back to its mother. You're almost part of the family now! What a great article you'll be able to do for your magazine.

The End

You stare at the strange man, who is standing still and looking stunned. Then you raise your camera. The man spins around and runs down the path. He must be a poacher!

Something makes you turn and look up the path. The hair on the back of your neck rises. Another man pokes his way through the bamboo onto the narrow path six feet in front of you. He's got a spear and a machete, too, and he's talking out loud as though he expected someone to be on the path. But not you!

You both stand motionless. You are close enough to see tiny flecks of rust on his deadly looking spearhead.

"Haooo!" The voice of the other poacher comes from the distance, calling his lost companion.

In an instant the man charges, thrusts his spear into your side, and flashes past you and Ed toward his friend.

You scream once with pain and shock. Ed and Mweri run to help you.

You scream again, longer this time, as Ed gently pulls the spear blade out.

Mweri quickly picks some special leaves and packs them around your wound. Then he makes a pillow for your head of wadded-up leaves tied with their own vines. You shut your eyes. You feel your camera at your side.

"Lucky you," says Ed. "That spear blade just missed your kidney! You'll be all right."

The End

You take a running start, jump—and just miss Ed's and Mweri's outstretched hands. As you jump for them, the ground beneath them crumbles into the deep, steam-filled crevasse.

The End

"Follow me!" you call to the others, leading them on all fours through the undergrowth. The wet green tunnel opens out onto a grassy place. You stop by a thick-trunked old tree.

"Look! Here she is!" you say. In the hollow trunk a little girl sits. She's in a gorilla nest! The trunk curves over it, protecting her from the rain.

"There you are! How did you get here? What happened to you?" her father asks and picks her up.

"That nest is a fresh one, I think," Ed says. "I wonder how she got here."

"Maybe gorillas found her and protected her while they rested here," you say. "Who knows?"

The girl holds on to her father and smiles. She's too young to say much.

"Thanks for finding our girl! Come back to our village with us. We'll have a celebration!" the men say.

That night around the fires after the celebration feast, everyone talks about the mystery of the lost girl.

"I was wrong about the gorillas," says her father. "I think they helped my daughter! They are our friends now. We'll share this forest with them."

The End

"If we go north and then climb east along that ridge you can see, I think we'll find the gorillas up there," Mweri says.

"Then let's start!" you answer.

From the forestry outpost, the trail winds higher to the north. As you turn east and climb the ridge that runs between two peaks, the trees become short and scattered, and the air gets cold and misty. Mweri points out giant groundsels, flowering plants over ten feet tall that look as if they belong in the desert. They disappear into the fog that's rolling in.

Mweri stops. "Some gorillas ahead! I've never seen them so high in the mountains. This isn't where I thought we'd find them at all!"

You look ahead but see nothing. Then, in a break in the fog, you see a line of black backs moving slowly across the trail going up the ridge to the mountain.

Mweri continues along the trail after he thinks the last gorilla has crossed. As you reach the crossing spot, another gorilla appears in the path right in front of you! You're so close you notice the dew clinging to the animal's fur. It's the leader of the group, a silverback male bringing up the rear of his group. The dew makes him look magnificent—silver all over. Without a sound the gorilla stares you in the eye, then turns and moves up the mountain.

Turn to page 83.

Word comes from park headquarters that Mweri has taken Ed to Kisoro, the nearest town, for treatment of the infection that's developed in his wound. You're on your own!

The gorilla group stays in the area. You make contact with them day after day. Contact consists of locating the group early each morning and then carefully approaching them in a crouched position pretending to eat the plants they're eating. Then you quietly stay right where they can watch *you*. The[illegible]re three babies with their mothers, two young black males, and the group's silverback leader: nine gorillas.

A cold rain drizzles into the forest. You shiver and try to keep your camera dry. You're hiding and watching the gorilla group as they try to keep out of the rain under the trunk of a huge leaning tree. All of you are wet and cold. Maybe you should make a shelter for yourself. You don't want to scare the gorillas, though.

If you make a shelter from the rain,
turn to page 52.

If you wait for the rain to pass, turn to page 7.

"Hello!" you greet the man, holding your hands out, palms open. "What are you hunting?"

"Deer," he answers. "We were coming to check our snares, and we heard those screams."

The bamboo trees rustle and click behind the man. A second poacher forces his way through the close-growing bamboo trees, spear first! He nods to you and joins his companion.

You look at them. "Your deer snare just caught and wounded a gorilla. Hunting is illegal in this forest! Are any hunters catching gorillas?"

They stare silently at the ground.

"Listen," you say. "We're trying to help the gorillas keep a small part of their forest. Tell us what you know, and we won't bother you."

The first poacher looks at you. "Yesterday two hunters showed us a baby gorilla they caught somewhere."

"Let's try to find those poachers!" you blurt out to Ed and Mweri. "Maybe we can rescue that baby gorilla and find out what happened to its family group!"

They nod, and you study the deer poachers. Can you trust them to take you to the gorilla poachers? Or should you ask them for directions and try to find the gorilla poachers on your own?

If you offer to pay these deer poachers to guide you to the gorilla poachers, turn to page 106.

If you just ask them for directions to the gorilla poachers, turn to page 46.

"Look at him!" says Ed. *Thwack! Thwack! Thwack!* "He's beating his chest! I think he's challenging the silverback in our group!"

"There he goes, Ed!" you say. The huge silverback crashes into the group you've been photographing. The two young males roar and jump on him. The lone silverback shakes them off and runs over to a baby. He grabs it and shakes it roughly, dropping it just in time to avoid the silverback leader and baby's mother, who charge him in a fury of screams and roars. Then he turns and crashes out of sight. You've caught some of the action with your camera.

"Ed, what if that strange silverback comes again? Maybe he'll hurt one of the babies! Let's try to scare him out of this group's territory," you say.

"It's natural for this challenging to happen," Ed insists.

"That new silverback wants some of this group to start his own family," Mweri adds.

You wonder about it. There are so few mountain gorillas left! Should you interfere and stop the fight?

If you remain in hiding and watch,
turn to page 112.

If you try to scare the strange silverback away,
turn to page 81.

"It's too risky to jump, Ed!" you yell. "I'll try to get around it. Stay with me!"

The ground shakes and you feel dizzy. With each tremor, the crack widens, and steam rushes up from it. It's widened into a crevasse in places, and clumps of earth large enough to hold trees tip slowly, silently into the steamy trench.

You find a place to join the others several hundred yards downhill. You're lucky!

"Mweri, you were right about the volcano! Let's get out of here!" you shout.

Turn to page 113.

The startled baby drops the frog and scampers away.

"Wild bush pigs on the trail!" calls Mweri. He's positioned near the trail.

You reach him in time to watch the group's silverback leader make a rush at the bush pigs. They grunt angrily and turn and run away. The big gorilla and the pigs running away with their tails in the air make a comic photograph.

"He's just making sure," Mweri says. "Bush pigs and gorillas don't harm each other."

"You're sure of that, Mweri? I'm going to quote you as an expert on bush pigs in this article I'm writing for *African Naturalist*. Hey, let me take your picture, too!" You point your camera at him.

The End

You follow Mweri quietly along the trail. No more deer snares appear.

"Aiiii! Aiiii!" The screams are violent. They come from up ahead.

Filled with dread, the three of you crawl toward the noise. Then you see a heaving swirl of black backs crowding around something in the middle of the trail. Horrifying, powerful screams and grunts come from the center of the group.

The gorilla leader forces his way into the cluster. You get glimpses of his silver back and head. He's standing, reaching high to chew something. It's a wire! One end leads to a thick bamboo pole, bent almost double. The other end encircles a gorilla's arm. The elastic force of the pole has yanked the frantic animal's arm up high above his head. The silverback is trying to cut the wire with his teeth!

His head moves up and down with the chewing motion. You photograph it with your telephoto equipment. Finally the wire releases with a snap, and the gorillas scatter.

You stand up and turn to Ed. "That gorilla was caught—!"

There's a movement behind Ed. A strange man steps onto the trail. He holds a spear in his right hand and a machete in his left! Is he a poacher coming to check his traps? You can't be sure. How should you greet him?

If you say "Hello!" and hold your hands out in greeting, turn to page 92.

If you say nothing, turn to page 86.

You walk toward the clearing where you hear the voices.

"Hey! Hello! Where'd you come from?" A tall, bearded man with a movie camera slung on his back greets you.

You shake hands. "I'm studying and photographing gorillas for *African Naturalist* magazine," you answer, smiling.

The other four, two men and two women, crowd around you. They've taken off their heavy packs and are all talking at once.

"Our guide left us this morning."

"I'm cold! Is it always raining in this place?"

"We're trying to get footage for a British Broadcasting Company TV program."

"Halvorsen at the park said you might—"

"Wait!" you interrupt, holding up your hands. "Slow down!"

You wish these TV people had never gotten past Halvorsen at the park headquarters. Without a guide, they're helpless and may even frighten the gorillas out of the Impenetrable Forest.

Perhaps you can get them to help *you*—that's the surest way to keep them from frightening the gorillas. But will they agree to it? Maybe you should offer *them* your help. They'll almost certainly accept, and you'll have some chance to protect the gorillas from them.

If you offer to help them, turn to page 72.

If you ask them to help you, turn to page 82.

Firmly you pull your camera away from the young gorilla's outstretched hand. It shrieks and rips at the vegetation in frustration. Still crying and fussing, it runs to its mother, who hugs it.

The two young males have been watching you. They move between you and the others. When you raise your camera to photograph them, they stare back. Behind them the group moves off in search of its afternoon food. The two gorillas guard the path when you attempt to follow. Their stares warn you not to approach closer. After a number of tries to renew friendly contact, you have to give up.

The End

As you wait in the heavy rain, the swirling water rises an inch on the wheels of the Land Rover.

The vehicle nears; it's big, whatever it is. The headlights are high up, and the motor sounds like a big-displacement diesel. It's revving fast in super-low gear.

When the vehicle pauses at the water's edge, you see that it's some type of a large truck. It starts slowly across the flooded section of road. Water swirls high on the truck as it barges through the deepest part. The headlights catch your Land Rover. You wave, and the truck stops.

"Hey, want a tow across?" a voice yells.

"Sure, I've got a tow chain here," you shout.

The truck turns around and stops in front of the Land Rover so you can hook the chain up. The water is so deep that it covers your headlights as you are dragged through the flooded road.

On the other side, you start the motor, unhook the chain, and run up to the cab of the truck. The light from your Land Rover reveals that it's an ancient all-wheel drive military transporter. "Thanks! Some rain! Never could have made it without your help. Are you headed to Kisoro?" you say.

"Yes!" a man's voice shouts over the diesel's rattle. "Rest of the road's clear; you won't have any trouble."

"Great. Thanks again," you say and wave.

You glimpsed the driver. His hair was long and pure white, his face so old! You make it safely back to park headquarters that night; all the way you think of the strange man who rescued you.

The End

"Thanks for the invitation, Halvorsen," you say. "But we're late to pick up Mweri at the forestry outpost. We have to leave now. And thanks for the bed last night. We'll check back with you as soon as we can. See you later!"

Two hours later you and Ed pull up to an orderly compound on the right-hand side of the road. A sign on the lawn says, "Uganda Forestry Outpost, Impenetrable Forest."

A man runs toward you. It's Mweri!

The three of you greet one another, and you explain about the roadblock that delayed you and Ed. "Any signs of gorillas, Mweri?" you ask.

"I took a hike toward the Zaire border west of here." He points to a mountain range behind the outpost. "I saw some gorilla signs. I found night nests just a day old in the forest on the edge of that volcano on the Zaire border. They might have headed north from there. I would need to see that area again to be certain."

"Let's explore that area first!" you answer.

Mweri kicks at the dirt. "I'm afraid to go to that place! I met some hunters from Zaire who were poaching deer and wild bush pigs. They told me they'd just seen steam coming from the ground!"

"Mweri, for years hot springs and geysers have bubbled up near that volcano," replies Ed. "It's nothing new."

If you say, "Look, Mweri, let's go back where you found those nests!" *turn to page 110.*

If you say, "Okay, Mweri. Let's head north of the volcano," *turn to page 90.*

It's Ed! Forgetting the gorillas, you leap up and run in the direction of his cries. The silverback roars in alarm at you. The screams of frightened gorillas fade behind you as you run toward Ed in the bamboo grove.

Poor Ed! He's hanging upside down just off the ground. A wire noose, attached to a strong bamboo spring pole, encircles one of his legs. He dangles helplessly above the trail. The wire has cut into his calf. Blood from the wound is dripping down onto his shirt and into his face. He reaches a hand out to you. "Help!"

Grabbing his body to save him from hitting the ground, you sever the wire from the pole with your machete and lower him gently.

"That's the most powerful snare I've ever seen! Just my luck to get caught!" Ed groans. You clean his wound and help him back to the forestry station, where, luckily, Mweri is waiting for you.

"Ed, take the Land Rover back to park headquarters and get your wound fixed—report those poachers, too! You'd better drive, Mweri. I'll stay and make contact with the gorillas again. I want them to get used to me so I can get closer."

Turn to page 91.

You decide you'd be better off waiting for Mweri. The early morning sun disappears in the fog that settles on the slopes of the nearby mountain, and mist begins to fall. Common weather in this high, tropical rain forest.

Now it's midmorning. Water drips from the Spanish moss that hangs from the branches of the *Hagenia* trees at the edge of the clearing. You and Ed pace the grounds of the outpost. You keep watching the trail for Mweri.

Suddenly you jump because Mweri has appeared next to you without a sound! Just like him.

You laugh. "Hi, Mweri! You scared me," you say.

"I was waiting here for you yesterday evening. Then some men came—not from my tribe. I camped up on that ridge for the night to keep away from them. But I heard them talk about catching a baby gorilla for a zoo! They are poachers!"

Mweri leads you and Ed into the forest. You follow him when he leaves the trail. The vegetation and vines are so thick and entwined that you have to climb up and over them to move forward.

You climb down into a steep-sided ravine. Up on the other side is a forest of thick-trunked trees with massive lower branches and strange, lovely red blossoms.

Mweri sniffs. You smell it, too, a musky sweet smell.

"Gorilla!" Ed says quietly. "They're somewhere in this *Hagenia* forest!"

Turn to page 67.

Back at the camp, Halvorsen shouts at Jonathan, "What? After a baby gorilla for a zoo? I can't believe it! We went through that once, and I said, 'Okay, you can keep your job!' But now you're under arrest, and you're going to jail!"

"Look, it's okay, Halvorsen—" you begin.

"Listen, I'm really sorry about this," Halvorsen cuts in. "I made a mistake giving this guy a second chance! He's made a mess of things!"

"Well," Ed adds, "that does it. We'll have to stop trying to make contact with this gorilla group, or they'll leave this last protected area."

Your adventure is over.

The End

You tell the poachers you'll pay them to guide you to the men.

The first poacher nods to you. "We will do this if you pay us now."

You make a deal. The two men set a fast pace down into the saddle area between the mountain you are on and the next one. The forest there has lots of *Hypericum* and *Hagenia* trees. Gorilla groups like to feed on the bark, nuts, and some leaves of these trees, as well as the ferns and orchids that grow on them.

Your guides head west toward the Uganda-Zaire border. Late in the afternoon one of them points to a grassy clearing below the bluff he's standing on.

"See the smoke? That's their camp," he says.

You all creep closer to the camp. Two men crouch in front of a smoky fire. One man is skinning a small animal. His companion is using a machete to whittle a wooden spit for cooking the meat. As you watch, the first man takes the spit and jams the carcass onto it.

"We'll wait till after dark, then we'll surprise them! We're five against two," you say.

In the dark the poachers' campfire sends sparks into their shelter, the hollow trunk of a tree.

Go on to the next page.

"Now!" you shout. The five of you rush the poachers' camp. Before they have a chance to move, you and Ed have grabbed their spears and machetes. Your hunter guides tie them up. Both men are scarcely larger than pygmies. They wear clothing made of skins and feathers. They tremble and moan as you and Ed question them about the baby gorilla. They're too frightened to talk!

You photograph everything in the camp: the smoked deer meat the men have, their snares and spears, and the skins they've hung on poles to dry.

Next morning you all search for some sign of the captured baby gorilla. No luck!

You look at the two poachers you've caught and feel sorry for them. "Ed, look at them!" you say. "They're so frightened!"

"We'd better get them to the Gorilla Sanctuary Park authorities while they have the strength to walk," Ed says.

"I'm going to stay and search for the baby," you say.

Ed and Mweri leave with the other men. Suddenly it's so quiet! The ashes of the dead fire blow in a gentle breeze.

"Eeeee! Eeeee!" A thin wailing sound comes from the forest. Your heart pounds. It could be the gorilla baby!

Turn to page 68.

The light is coming from a poacher's camp! You stop the Land Rover. From it you can see right into the camp, a couple of hundred yards down the steep, wooded slope. By the light of the campfire, you see that the poachers are using a *Hagenia* tree as shelter for the night. One man is sleeping against the tree trunk, a second one by the fire. The second man sits up suddenly and stares in the direction of your headlights.

"Those poachers are camping and hunting in this protected area!" you exclaim.

"I know," replies Ed. "They're getting bolder and bolder."

You shift into first gear and continue up the trail. Nervous and exhausted, you and Ed reach the forestry outpost an hour later. There's no sign of Mweri inside the empty cottage. By the light of a kerosene lamp, you both roll out your sleeping bags on cots.

At daylight Ed searches the area for Mweri, while you look at a map of the forest.

"No sign he's been here," Ed reports. "Want to wait to see if he shows up?"

You've been depending on having Mweri along on your expedition. He's the best gorilla tracker you know, and until now he's been reliable. You and Ed *can* track gorillas on your own, though, and you want to start!

If you decide to wait for Mweri,
turn to page 104.

If you decide to start without him,
turn to page 4.

Mweri looks up at you. "All right, we'll look at the nests. But let's be careful when we get near the volcano."

Mweri leads the way up a steep trail away from the forestry outpost. It's hard to keep up with him. After hours of climbing, he stops to show you a view to the west. He points and says, "Zaire is about half a mile that way. It's too high here for villagers. No one lives here. Only hunters come here."

"How much farther to where you saw the gorillas' nests?" you ask wearily.

"Not far. We have to climb a little more to get over this ridge and past the volcano. About an hour more."

At the ridge's high point, the gray, pumicelike stone is fine and slippery underfoot.

You stop for a snack of bread and dried meat. At first you think your weight has somehow shifted the boulder you're sitting on. It is moving and trembling! Mweri and Ed jump off and run along the trail. You stay on the boulder.

"Hurry! Let's go!" Ed calls to you.

Turn to page 114.

You decide to stay in your road camp, and Halvorsen and Jonathan leave.

At dawn you and Ed get started. You make a turn at a sign for the Impenetrable Forest outpost. An hour later you are there. Mweri runs out of the outpost building at the sight of the Land Rover.

"Sorry we're late, Mweri! We had trouble with a roadblock yesterday," you greet him. You and Ed climb out of the Land Rover. "Let's get going and see if gorillas have really migrated to the Impenetrable Forest!"

"First let's check the far slope of the mountain up there," Mweri says, pointing. "There's a bamboo grove just coming into shoots. They go for that!"

It's a hard climb, scrabbling over the volcanic rock high up the mountain. Mweri never seems to tire as he works around the mountain to the bamboo forest. Suddenly he freezes.

"They're here! Gorillas!" he whispers over his shoulder. "Keep down!"

You and Ed crawl on all fours behind Mweri. He follows an animal trail along the edge of the bamboo. The slender bamboo trees are so close together that nothing else grows among them.

"Mweri, look!" You touch his shoulder and point to a single strand of thin wire hanging from a bamboo pole by the trail.

"Piece of a deer snare," he whispers. "Deer poachers. Bad luck!"

Turn to page 97.

You crouch down to watch and wait. The group calms down. The silverback leader and the two young males move out of sight. In an opening two females are expertly stripping *Galium* leaves, a favorite food, from their vines, wadding them up, and popping them into their mouths. They've seen you before and pay no attention. Behind some vegetation one of the baby gorillas is playing, jumping up and down on something you can't see.

The gorillas move on, disappearing on the far side of the opening. Ed and Mweri follow them, pretending to eat *Galium* leaves to reassure them.

You take a minute to change your lens and load up with film.

There are gorilla screams up ahead! Thrashing sounds come from the undergrowth. After a silence you hear chest beatings and hootings. Forgetting to crouch down, you run toward the sound. Ed and Mweri are poking at something on the ground.

"I think that silverback intruder killed this baby female!" Ed points at a tousled, furry black heap.

"I can't understand it!" you say. "It's so cruel."

"He could have been frustrated because he was alone," Ed says softly. "But it's sad. So few gorillas left, and this little one is killed before she had a chance."

"Poor little thing. I was just trying to photograph her playing back there in the *Galium* vines," you say. To keep busy, you take pictures of the dead baby and of Mweri, who's digging a tiny grave with his machete.

The End

At a safe distance from the volcano, Mweri stops under a *Hagenia* tree. Its trunk is huge and has a deep recess. You all lie down in the shelter of the hollow to rest. It's midafternoon. This is a good place to camp, not too far from the gorilla nests Mweri spotted.

Without meaning to, you doze off. When you wake up, Mweri and Ed are napping near you. You get up to stretch your legs.

A short walk along the trail there's a grassy meadow, cleared of all trees and bushes. It's bowl shaped and about the size of a basketball court.

Curious, you walk to its edge. Something is peculiar about it: the grass looks unusually green and rich, and a delicate, foggy haze hangs over the meadow. The haze hangs thickest in the center, which is the low point. It's beautiful—and mysteriously peaceful.

You are caught in its spell. You notice the soft outlines of animal forms in the thick fog: a wild bush pig, a couple of deer. For a second you think they're asleep.

They're dead! You spy more animal corpses. Some seem to be half melted into the ground, with fur hanging from their naked white rib bones.

What's happened? Maybe you should wake up Ed and Mweri. Is this a mysterious burial ground?

If you get Ed and Mweri before you explore this meadow, turn to page 51.

If you explore the meadow right now, turn to page 34.

Too late! Steam spurts out of the ground in a line that cuts right across your path to Ed and Mweri. Along that line, vegetation and trees start moving and swaying—but there's no breeze! The ground underfoot is shaking, and you feel sick from the motion. Things look out of focus, too, because everything is vibrating. Geysers of steam boil out of new places along the crack.

The crack separating you from the others is now a foot wide, and as you watch, trees and shrubs sink into the steaming trench. It's growing wider! Maybe you can run around it—but it's getting longer, too!

"Hurry! Jump! You can make it!" Ed shouts and holds out his hand.

But the crack is even wider now.

If you try to jump to them, turn to page 87.

If you try to run around the crack, turn to page 95.

"Hi!" you say to the two men. "Are you from the Gorilla Sanctuary? I'm on the way to the Impenetrable Forest to look for mountain gorillas. My partner, Ed Kiwanuka, and I ran into this roadblock earlier today. We're camped up the road there."

The taller man says, "Kiwanuka? He's an old friend of mine!" Then he introduces himself. "I'm Per Halvorsen, warden of Kigezi Gorilla Sanctuary Park. And this is Jonathan, one of my park rangers."

You invite them back to your camp, and the three of you drive there in Halvorsen's truck.

Halvorsen is delighted to see his old friend, Ed. "Come to my place at park headquarters for the night," he says to you and Ed. "We can talk about the gorillas. In the morning I'll show you a special mountain trail that goes to the Impenetrable Forest."

You wonder. Halvorsen's offer is tempting, and he might help your expedition find the gorillas. But going to park headquarters will take you farther away from the outpost where Mweri, your tracker, is waiting. You need Mweri, and you're already late to meet him.

If you accept Halvorsen's offer to stay at park headquarters, turn to page 5.

If you stay in your own camp, turn to page 111.

Slipping on the wet trail, you run for your life. The water buffalo's hooves beat the trail so hard you can feel the thumps!

You lunge for a branch that hangs over the trail. *Smash!* Too late! A horn rips your right thigh and flings you down onto the trail!

"Help, help!" you scream in agony. You crawl a few feet. The water buffalo stares and paws the mud.

"No!" you shout. The animal charges again, rears up, and stabs its front horns into your body again and again. Blood flows from your broken body and mixes with the red watery mud.

The End

You tell Ed the story and show him the article about Surprise that you're writing for *African Naturalist.*

"That's great!" he says. "It should get some support for protecting the gorillas in this forest from poachers. What about Surprise herself?"

"Let's take her back into the wild! She's ready to join a real gorilla family now. How about starting to find one for her tomorrow morning?" you say.

Ed looks at Surprise. She's asleep in a nest she's made from some of your clothes and papers.

He chuckles. "If she only knew the big adventure she's going to have tomorrow," he says.

The End

You tug frantically at the door handle before the dusty air you sucked in makes you cough. For a moment you feel pain and terror as your lungs fill with water. You struggle for a moment, but it's no use. Then you relax.

Minutes later the driver of an approaching vehicle, a military transporter, sees an eerie underwater glow coming from the still-burning lights of your submerged Land Rover.

The End